1985

THE YEAR
I WAS BORN

A Daily Record of Events
Canadian Edition

Compiled by PAT HANCOCK
Illustrated by BILL SLAVIN

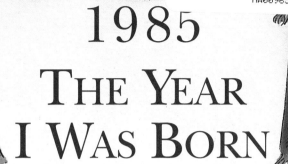

BIRTH CERTIFICATE

Name: _____

Birthdate: _____

Time: _____

Place: _____

Weight: _____

Length: _____

Mother's name: _____

Father's name: _____

Kids Can Press Ltd.
Toronto

With thanks to Linda Granfield for her generous support, and to Ron and Michael for their humour and patience during months of living with someone stricken by research madness.

Printed by permission of Signpost Books, Ltd., England

First Canadian edition published 1996

Canadian Cataloguing in Publication Data

Hancock, Pat
      1985, the year I was born : a daily record of events

Canadian ed.
ISBN 1-55074-308-2

1. Nineteen eighty-five, A.D. — Chronology — Juvenile literature.
2. Canada — History — 1963—　　　 — Chronology — Juvenile literature.*
I. Slavin, Bill.　II. Title.

FC630.H35　1995　　　j971.064'7　　　C95-931860-7
F1034.2.H35　1995

Kids Can Press Ltd.
29 Birch Avenue
Toronto, Ontario, Canada
M4V 1E2

Edited by Trudee Romanek
Designed by Esperança Melo
Printed and bound in Hong Kong

96　0 9 8 7 6 5 4 3 2 1

A Week of Birthdays

Monday's child is fair of face,
Tuesday's child is full of grace,
Wednesday's child is full of woe,
Thursday's child has far to go,
Friday's child is loving and giving,
Saturday's child works hard for its living,
But the child that's born on the Sabbath day
Is bonny and blithe, and good and gay.

The Days of the Week

Sunday — the sun's day

Monday — the moon's day

Tuesday — day of Tiu, or Tyr, the Norse god of war and the sky

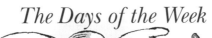

Wednesday — Woden's day (Woden, or Odin, was the chief Norse god)

Thursday — Thor's day (in Norse mythology, Thor was the god of thunder)

Friday — Freya's day (Freya was a wife of Odin and the goddess of love and beauty)

Saturday — Saturn's day (in Roman mythology, Saturn was a harvest god)

The Months

January — the month of Janus, Roman god of doorways, who had two faces looking in opposite directions

February — the month of februa, a Roman festival of purification

March — the month of Mars, the Roman god of war

April — the month of Venus, the Roman goddess of love

May — the month of Maia, the Roman goddess of spring

June — the month of Juno, the principal Roman goddess

July — the month of Roman emperor Julius Caesar

August — the month of Roman emperor Augustus

September — the seventh (*septem*) month of the old Roman calendar

October — the eighth (*octo*) month of the old Roman calendar

November — the ninth (*novem*) month of the old Roman calendar

December — the tenth (*decem*) month of the old Roman calendar

JVLIVS   AVGVSTVS

Birthstones and Flowers

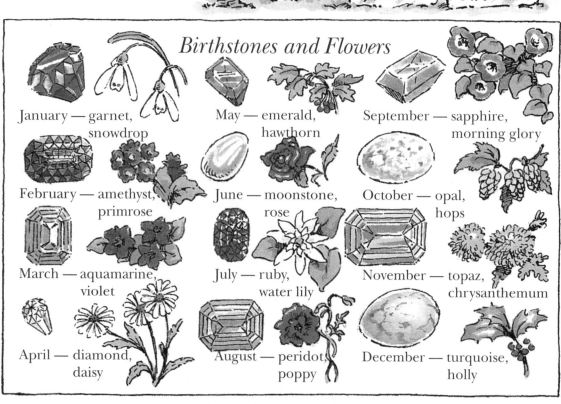

January — garnet, snowdrop

February — amethyst, primrose

March — aquamarine, violet

April — diamond, daisy

May — emerald, hawthorn

June — moonstone, rose

July — ruby, water lily

August — peridot, poppy

September — sapphire, morning glory

October — opal, hops

November — topaz, chrysanthemum

December — turquoise, holly

Extra! Extra!

CP's Game Plan

Find a long plane trip boring? Canadian Pacific may have just what you are looking for. It's installing 7000 video games on 36 of its planes. The games are on trays that pop down from the back of the seat in front of you. CP plans to charge $3–$5 an hour to rent the games.

Canada's First Stamp

The Three-Penny Beaver was first issued on April 23, 1851. Just 150 200 copies of the stamp were printed. It was designed by Sir Sandford Fleming, the inventor of Standard Time. In mint condition this stamp sells for at least $10 000.

Trivia tidbit

More than one million youngsters in Canada play minor league hockey.

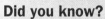

Did you know?

"First foot" or *qual-tagh* is still a popular custom in Scotland and parts of Britain.

According to the custom, it is good luck to have a tall, dark-haired man as the first visitor of the new year, so people will often make sure that a brown- or black-haired friend or relative is the first person to set foot in their homes just after midnight.

What's *that?!?* Matrioska

New Year's is a special day for children in Russia. It's customary for Grandfather Frost to bring them toys and candies on this day. One of the favourite toys he and his helpers give out is a *matrioska* or "little mother" doll. This toy is actually a collection of several hollow wooden dolls that nestle inside one another.

JANUARY

Tuesday 1
New Year's Day
Five scuba divers take a midnight dip in the icy waters of the St. Lawrence River to explore an old shipwreck at Cardinal, Ontario.
☆ **1950** — birth of Philippe Beha, illustrator of *What Do the Fairies Do with All Those Teeth?*

Wednesday 2
Prince racks up ten American Music Award nominations. Anne Murray is nominated for four awards in the country music category.
☆ **1939** — birth of Jean Little, author of *The Revenge of the Small Small*

Thursday 3
In Britain, a 20-year-old man who had been blind for five years can now see. His eyesight returned when he woke up after having surgery to remove two wisdom teeth.
☆ **1939** — birth of Bobby Hull, hockey player

Friday 4
Thanks to a $70 million private donation, a telescope powerful enough to see a glowing fridge light bulb as far away as the moon will be built on the top of a volcanic mountain in Hawaii.
☆ **1926** — birth of Betty Kennedy, broadcaster–T.V. personality

Saturday 5
The American Bus Association puts the Abbotsford, British Columbia, air show at the top of its list of recommended events for bus-travellers planning vacations this year.
☆ **1829** — birth of William Mellis Christie, biscuit maker

Sunday 6
It's definitely a bad weather day. A winter storm shuts down much of Atlantic Canada. In Europe, people are skiing on Rome's streets and making snowmen in front of Buckingham Palace.

Monday 7
The University of British Columbia is looking for good homes, complete with blueberries and salmon, for two grizzly bears whose research careers have ended.
☆ **1827** — birth of Sir Sandford Fleming, inventor, scientist, railway surveyor and engineer

Tuesday 8
Elvis fans are in seventh heaven as Priscilla Presley takes them on a video tour of the King's Graceland mansion.
☆ **1945** — birth of sports announcer Dave Hodge

Wednesday 9
Hundreds of young trees are arriving in Vancouver to landscape next year's Expo '86 site. The forest-filled province had to buy the trees from nurseries in Chicago.
☆ **1963** — birth of Larry Cain, Olympic gold-medal canoeist

Thursday 10
Europe is caught in the grip of a cold snap. The monkeys at Germany's Frankfurt Zoo are even suffering from frostbite.
☆ **1935** — birth of "Rompin' Ronnie" Hawkins, singer-songwriter

JANUARY

Friday 11
The VCR trend keeps growing. The price of these new toys has dropped to about $500 from $1000 two years ago. Video stores can't keep up with the Friday night crowds looking for movies to rent.
☆ 1815 — birth of Sir John A. Macdonald, first prime minister of Canada
☆ 1934 — birth of Jean Chrétien, 20th prime minister of Canada

Saturday 12
Ottawa's Tina Takahashi is Canada's athlete of the month. At the university championships in December, Takahashi became the first Canadian ever to win a world judo competition.
☆ 1955 — birth of Kim LaFave, illustrator of *I Am Small*

Sunday 13
The most watched T.V. show in Canada this past week was *Dallas* on CBC. "The Thornbirds" miniseries was No. 1 for CTV, Global's top show was *Dynasty*, and *Poivre et Sel* headed the ratings list for Radio Canada.
☆ 1933 — birth of Paige Brydon, ballet dancer, choreographer and director

Monday 14
Bell Canada is cracking down on a new breed of thieves — computer hackers who are illegally making long-distance phone calls.
☆ 1935 — birth of Lucille Wheeler, champion alpine skier

Tuesday 15
School boards offer parents courses on how to teach their kids to use home computers. Boy, do they have *that* backwards.
☆ 1947 — birth of Veronica Tennant, ballet dancer

Wednesday 16
A severe winter storm hits Goose Bay, Labrador, dumping 71 cm of snow on the town.
☆ 1874 — birth of Robert Service, poet of the Yukon

Thursday 17
One-legged runner Steve Fonyo cries when he spots Native schoolchildren waiting in the freezing cold to welcome him to Manitoba.
☆ 1929 — birth of Jacques Plante, hockey goaltender

Friday 18
Ontario's Premier William Davis announces that Toronto will get a $150 million domed stadium with a retractable roof.
☆ 1950 — birth of Gilles Villeneuve, auto racer

Saturday 19
Warning! The current breakdancing fad can be back-breaking. The *New England Journal of Medicine* says doctors are seeing patients who have serious spinal injuries as a result.
☆ 1934 — birth of Lloyd Robertson, T.V. news anchor

Sunday 20
It's Super Bowl XIX Sunday in Palo Alto, California. The San Francisco 49ers are the big winners, trouncing the Miami Dolphins 38–16. Members of the winning team each collect $36 000.
☆ 1921 — birth of Jacques Ferron, doctor and founder of the Rhinoceros Party

JANUARY

Monday 21
Ronald Reagan re-enacts taking the oath of office for the television cameras. Not too many people would have watched the real presidential swearing-in ceremony yesterday, with the Super Bowl going on.
☆ 1937 — birth of Jim Unger, cartoonist and creator of "Herman"

Tuesday 22
Freezing temperatures have damaged 90 per cent of Florida's grapefruit and orange crop, so growers are lined up at the juice factories. That's all the damaged fruit is good for now.
☆ 1957 — birth of Mike Bossy, hockey player

Wednesday 23
The Quebec Cabinet votes to complete the Olympic Stadium's retractable roof at a cost of an additional $71 million.
☆ 1929 — birth of John Polanyi, Nobel Prize co-winner in chemistry

Thursday 24
The federal government wants to permit the use of imperial as well as metric units, instead of completely switching over to the metric system as originally planned.
☆ 1942 — birth of Sandy Frances Duncan, author of *Listen to Me, Grace Kelly*

Friday 25
Canadians may soon be saying farewell to the dollar bill. A federal committee is studying the possibility of replacing it with a dollar coin.
☆ 1959 — birth of Nicola Morgan, author-illustrator of *Once in a Blue Moon*

Saturday 26
Ontario delivers 30 moose to Michigan. In return, Michigan will soon be giving Ontario 150 wild turkeys.
☆ 1961 — birth of Wayne Gretzky, hockey player

Sunday 27
Twenty-two-year-old freestyle skier Lloyd Langlois of Magog, Quebec, is the new men's world aerials champion.
☆ 1931 — birth of Mordecai Richler, author of *Jacob Two-Two and the Dinosaur*

Monday 28
A star-studded cast of musical artists records the Lionel Ritchie–Michael Jackson song, "We Are the World." Profits from sales will go towards emergency famine relief in Africa.
☆ 1822 — birth of Alexander Mackenzie, second prime minister of Canada

Tuesday 29
Madonna's "Like a Virgin" has topped the charts every week this month.
☆ 1901 — birth of Edward Plunkett "E.P." Taylor, businessman and thoroughbred stable owner

Wednesday 30
Statistics Canada has finally removed pantsuits, home perms and black-and-white T.V.s from the shopping list it uses to estimate the average cost of living in Canada.
☆ 1914 — birth of John Ireland, actor

Thursday 31
A used Three-Penny Beaver stamp, one of the first stamps issued in Canada, has been sold at an auction for $577.
☆ 1964 — birth of Sylvie Bernier, Olympic gold-medal diver

FEBRUARY

Extra! Extra!

The Changing Face of South Africa

The new Anglican bishop of Johannesburg is the Right Reverend Bishop Desmond Tutu — the first black person appointed to such a position. In a ceremony rich with traditional African music, Bishop Tutu greeted his mainly white congregation with a challenge for all South Africans to work together for justice. Last year's winner of the Nobel Peace Prize, Bishop Tutu had to get special permission to go into the cathedral's white neighbourhood for the ceremony.

Food for Love

Chocolates have always been a popular gift on Valentine's Day. Scientists now say they've discovered a chemical in chocolate, especially the dark kind, that actually makes a person feel more romantic.

Trivia tidbit
Dr. Roberta Bondar devoured science fiction books as a youngster. She's also a *Star Trek* fan.

Did you know?
February 2 is Groundhog Day, the day we watch this little animal to find out when warm weather will arrive. But groundhogs weren't the original predictors of spring. They replaced badgers and hedgehogs when British settlers couldn't find any of those creatures in Canada.

What's *that?!?*   Bonhomme
Bonhomme Carnaval is the official mascot of the Quebec Winter Carnival. He's a large, jolly snowman who mingles with carnival visitors or welcomes them to his palace made of ice and snow. *Bonhomme de neige* means "snowman" in French.

Friday 1
Canadian researchers say that the polluting effects of acid rain are even showing up in the high Arctic.
☆ **1882** — birth of Louis St. Laurent, 12th prime minister of Canada

Saturday 2
Groundhog Day
A great horned owl swoops down and attacks a couple cross-country skiing through the woods in Timmins, Ontario. Luckily, the skiers are okay.

Sunday 3
Linda Kennedy ends 440 hours of rocking in a rocking chair at a Calgary furniture store. That's one for the record books.
☆ **1936** — birth of "Stompin' Tom" Connors, singer-songwriter

FEBRUARY

Monday
4
Critics are surprised to learn that hockey commentator Don Cherry is gaining quite a fan following. Some predict his popularity won't last much longer.
☆ **1885** — birth of Cairine Reay Wilson, Canada's first woman senator

Tuesday
5
In keeping with its nuclear-free policy, New Zealand won't let ships into port unless assured that they aren't carrying nuclear weapons. The U.S. navy won't give out that information, so its ships have to sail on by.

Wednesday
6
A Soviet icebreaker is racing to free more than 1000 white whales trapped in ice near the Bering Strait.
☆ **1946** — birth of Kate McGarrigle, singer-songwriter

Thursday
7
Bonhomme greets visitors on opening day of Quebec City's annual winter carnival.
☆ **1968** — birth of Mark Tewksbury, Olympic gold-medal swimmer

Friday
8
Good news! A search-and-rescue plane spots four Cape Dorset hunters trapped on an ice floe. They were reported missing two days ago.

Saturday
9
At the Canadian figure skating championships in Moncton, New Brunswick, Brian Orser wins gold for the fifth year in a row.
☆ **1894** — birth of Billy Bishop, World War I pilot

Sunday
10
"Tears Are Not Enough" is recorded in a Toronto studio. Neil Young, Anne Murray, Bryan Adams, Paul Shaffer and Joni Mitchell are just a few of those gathered to raise money for the Ethiopian famine relief effort.
☆ **1964** — birth of Victor Davis, champion swimmer

Monday
11
Canadian swimmers have done it again. Both Alex Baumann and Mark Tewksbury won gold medals at an international meet in Bonn, West Germany, yesterday.

Tuesday
12
Canadian astronauts Roberta Bondar, Ken Money and Bob Thirsk are busy preparing. One of the three will be chosen for a 1986 shuttle flight.
☆ **1915** — birth of Lorne Greene, actor who played Pa in *Bonanza*

Wednesday
13
Toronto's 17-year-old Carling Bassett beats out Hana Mandlikova to make it to the semi-finals of the Lipton international tennis tournament.
☆ **1925** — birth of Gerald Tailfeathers, artist

Thursday
14
Valentine's Day
Bowser and Fifi can have a romantic dinner on opening day at Montreal's À Rebrousse poil — a restaurant for dogs!
☆ **1931** — birth of Dorothy Joan Harris, author of *The Case of the Mystery Note*

Friday
15
Moscow chess officials call off the world championship. Karpov and Kasparov have played 48 games over the last six months and are just too tired to go on.

Saturday
16
Jason Atkins, 13, of Willowdale, Ontario, racks up a record 102 million points on the video game Joust. It cost him $25 to play for 36 hours.

Sunday
17
At a meet in Auckland, New Zealand's great middle-distance runner John Walker becomes the first athlete to run 100 sub-four-minute miles.

FEBRUARY

Monday
18

Heritage Day
During a private audience at the Vatican, Dene leaders invite the Pope back to Fort Simpson. His plane couldn't land there last September because of fog.
☆ **1933** — birth of Laszlo Gal, illustrator of *Pome and Peel*

Tuesday
19

Peter Gatien, owner of a New York night club, buys two more disco sites — in London and Chicago. Gatien's success began just nine years ago when he opened his first disco, the Aardvark, in his home town of Cornwall, Ontario.
☆ **1854** — birth of William Frederick King, astronomer

Wednesday
20

Chinese New Year
As the Year of the Ox begins, people celebrating in China are ignoring a government official's recent suggestion that knives and forks replace chopsticks.
☆ **1942** — birth of Phil Esposito, hockey player

Thursday
21

The Academy of Science Fiction, Fantasy and Horror Films nominates George Burns as best actor for playing God in *Oh God, You Devil*.
☆ **1963** — birth of Lori Fung, Olympic gold-medal gymnast

Friday
22

Canada's indoor speed skaters continue to shine at the Winter University Games in Italy. World champion Guy Daignault of Montreal wins the men's 1500 m and his younger brother Michel is third. Windsor's Maryse Perrault misses first place in the women's 1500 m by just 0.2 seconds.
☆ **1948** — birth of Paul Kropp, author of *Ellen/Elena/Luna*

Saturday
23

Canadian stamp collectors write letters objecting to the recent announcement that the National Postal Museum in Ottawa is about to be closed.
☆ **1949** — birth of Marc Garneau, first Canadian astronaut to go into space

Sunday
24

A shower of meteors streaks across the northern Alberta skies. Scientists speculate some may weigh thousands of kilograms.
☆ **1932** — birth of John Vernon, actor

Monday
25

Donald Brooks, a chemistry professor at the University of British Columbia, is pleased to learn that shuttle astronauts will carry out his team's microgravity experiments on living cells on the next shuttle flight, scheduled for March.
☆ **1752** — birth of John Graves Simcoe, governor of Upper Canada

Tuesday
26

Tara Smith, 12, is walking on stilts to keep dry as Chatham, Ontario, experiences its worst flood ever. Rain and melting snow have driven two Chatham creeks to levels 4.6 m above normal.
☆ **1928** — birth of Monique Leyrac, singer and actor

Wednesday
27

People living in a Victoria, British Columbia, suburb can be fined up to $500 for throwing newspapers in the garbage instead of recycling them.
☆ **1899** — birth of Charles H. Best, co-discoverer of insulin

Thursday
28

Parents are being warned not to give ASA to children and teens with fevers. There's a possible link between it and a condition called Rye's syndrome.
☆ **1973** — birth of Eric Lindros, hockey player

MARCH

Extra! Extra!

High Tech Affair

Expo '85 is under way in Tsukaba, Japan. The 40 or so countries with pavilions at the fair are displaying all sorts of electronic gadgets. There's a handheld computer that translates a conversation you're having with someone who speaks another language, and there's a robot that paints your portrait. Big doesn't begin to describe the skyscraper-high ferris wheel or the Sony Jumbotron, a T.V. screen that would nearly fill four basketball courts. Organizers are hoping 20 million people will visit the fair during the next six months.

Academy Awards Winners

Millions of viewers around the world watched the film industry celebrate Oscar Night, the evening of the Academy Awards. The major winners were:

☆ Best Actor — William Hurt, in *Kiss of the Spider Woman*
☆ Best Actress — Geraldine Page, in *The Trip to Bountiful*
☆ Best Picture — *Out of Africa*

Trivia tidbit

On March 21, CBC Radio plays Bach all day long to celebrate the 300th anniversary of the composer's birth.

Did you know?

Mount Etna, Europe's highest and most active volcano, has erupted more than 250 times that we know of, and has been active for about 2 million years.

What's *that?!?* Canadarm

Because it was designed and built in Canada, the manipulator arm astronauts use to complete many tasks outside the space shuttle has been called the Canadarm. It's actually a robot 15 m long that's operated from a separate, or remote, computerized control panel.

MARCH

Friday 1
The Cold Lake Indian band in Alberta signs a $12 million deal with Husky Oil permitting oil and gas exploration on band land.
☆ 1947 — birth of Alan Thicke, comedian and actor

Saturday 2
At the third annual Harry Jerome Awards presentations, young black Canadians are honoured for their accomplishments. Top international sprinter Marita Payne is among those recognized.
☆ 1948 — birth of Camilla Gryski, author of *Camilla Gryski's Favourite String Games*

Sunday 3
Canadian freestyle skiers Lloyd Langlois and Merideth Gardner each win gold at a World Cup competition in West Germany.
☆ 1847 — birth of Alexander Graham Bell, inventor of the telephone

Monday 4
Chinese officials have banned all lotteries because they believe they "corrode" people's minds.
☆ 1901 — birth of Wilbur Franks, inventor of the "G suit," the prototype of the space suit

Tuesday 5
Montreal artist Jacques Payette wins the $10 000 first prize in the painting category of the McDonald's Restaurants of Canada fine-art competition.

Wednesday 6
Crowds cheer on Steve Fonyo as he braves the cold Saskatchewan weather. His Journey for Lives has raised $50 000 so far for cancer research.
☆ 1940 — birth of Ken Danby, artist

Thursday 7
Five-time Canadian champion Brian Orser wins silver at the world figure skating championships in Tokyo, Japan.
☆ 1934 — birth of Douglas Cardinal, world renowned Métis architect

Friday 8
Inco and Spar have agreed to work together on an underground version of the space manipulator arm — the Canadarm — for use in mining.
☆ 1896 — birth of Charlotte Whitton, Canada's first woman mayor (of Ottawa)

Saturday 9
East German figure skater Katarina Witt is the women's world champion for the second year in a row.
☆ 1934 — birth of Marlene Stewart Streit, champion golfer

Sunday 10
The southeast crater of Sicily's Mount Etna blows its top.
☆ 1947 — birth of Kim Campbell, 19th and first woman prime minister of Canada

Monday 11
Mikhail Gorbachev agrees to become the new General Secretary of the Communist Party, the most powerful position in the Soviet Republic.
☆ 1943 — birth of Sharon Siamon, author of *Gallop for Gold*

Tuesday 12
Calgary's Catholic school trustees vote on abolishing the strap. The strap wins 4–3.
☆ 1821 — birth of Sir John Abbot, third prime minister of Canada

MARCH

Wednesday 13

Ontario announces plans to twin with the province of Jiangsu in China and to build a science centre there similar to Toronto's Ontario Science Centre.

☆ **1914** — birth of W.O. Mitchell, author of *Who Has Seen the Wind*

Thursday 14

Drivers on Germany's autobahn (an expressway with no speed limit) slow down when they see fake speed limit signs put up by an environmental group concerned about the effect of exhaust pollution.

☆ **1968** — birth of Megan Follows, actor

Friday 15

Thousands of Torontonians eat cold dinners in the dark as a power blackout lasting more than an hour "switches off" the city's east end.

☆ **1943** — birth of David Cronenberg, film maker

Saturday 16

Tommy and Tulip are the proud parents of Patrick, an 8-kg baby tapir. The Metro Toronto Zoo's newest arrival is the third tapir born in Canada.

☆ **1946** — birth of Pat Hancock, author of this book

Sunday 17

St. Patrick's Day
Prime Minister Mulroney and President Reagan meet in Quebec for the Shamrock Summit. They discuss acid rain and sing Irish songs together.

☆ **1937** — birth of Aqjangajuk Shaa, stone carver

Monday 18

What's cool these days? *Decent, awesome, kickin' it, space cadet* and *giving static*. And *cool* is still cool. So is *bad*. They've both been hanging in there since the 1960s.

☆ **1871** — birth of Frederick Simpson Coburn, painter and illustrator

Tuesday 19

Flamingos running from a fire sweeping across Isabella, a Galapagos island, are losing their pink colour.

☆ **1942** — birth of Sonia Craddock, author of *Hal, the Third Class Hero*

Wednesday 20

Spring Equinox
Rearchers say spring fever is real. It's probably caused by a chemical reaction affected by day length, and it's not contagious.

☆ **1939** — birth of Brian Mulroney, 18th prime minister of Canada

Thursday 21

It's Genie Night in Canada. The film *Bad Boy* wins six awards, and Ivan Reitman is honoured for "outstanding contribution to the world of comedy" for his work on movies such as *Ghostbusters, Animal House* and *Stripes*.

☆ **1904** — birth of Jehane Benoît, author, cooking expert, and T.V. and radio personality

MARCH

Friday
22
Porky's Revenge! and *Friday the 13th Part V* open today. Also playing are *Baby, Mask, Last Dragon* and *The Care Bears Movie*.
☆ **1932** — birth of William Shatner, actor best known as Captain Kirk in *Star Trek*

Saturday
23
Thousands show up for free rides on the new LRT — Light Rapid Transit — line in Scarborough, Ontario.
☆ **1910** — birth of Harry Lambert Welsh, physicist

Sunday
24
Martina Navratilova wins again. This is her third Virginia Slims tennis championship in a row. She takes home $500 000 for this victory.
☆ **1890** — birth of Agnes Macphail, first woman elected to Canada's Parliament

Monday
25
Montrealer Jon Minnis's animated film *Charade* wins an Oscar at tonight's Academy Awards ceremonies. *Charade*, a college project, took $300 and three months to make. He got an A+ on it at school, too.

Tuesday
26
Cash registers are ringing as sales of the two-album soundtrack of *Amadeus* skyrocket. Too bad Mozart isn't around to collect a cut of the sales.
☆ **1963** — birth of Roch Voisine, singer-songwriter and radio and T.V. host

Wednesday
27
Hurray! Vancouver nutritionist Corrine Eisler says liver isn't on the eat-it—it's-good-for-you list any more. It's high in cholesterol and certain environmental pollutants that animals are exposed to.

Thursday
28
At the Metro Toronto Zoo, 4 moose, 13 elk and 43 bison are being kept in isolation after being exposed to wandering rabid foxes.
☆ **1951** — birth of Karen Kain, ballet dancer

Friday
29
Quebec's Pierre Harvey goes home from the Canadian senior cross-country skiing championships with three gold medals to add to his collection.
☆ **1956** — birth of Ted Staunton, author of *Anna Takes Charge*

Saturday
30
Canadian Olympic basketball player Bill Wennington takes on Patrick Ewing in an NCAA playoff between the St. John's Redmen and the Georgetown Hoyas.
☆ **1968** — birth of Céline Dion, singer

Sunday
31
Wrestlemania is a huge hit. The Executioner loses, the Giant flattens the Stud, and Hulk Hogan and Mr. T triumph over Rowdy Roddy and Mr. Wonderful.
☆ **1968** — birth of Maestro Fresh-Wes, rap artist

Extra! Extra!

Eleven Athletes Honoured

Eleven of Canada's great athletes have just been inducted into the Canadian Sports Hall of Fame.

Alex Baumann — swimmer
Sylvie Bernier — diver
Lisa Buscombe — field archer
Larry Cain — canoeist
Victor Davis — swimmer
Anne Ottenbrite — swimmer
Steve Podborski — downhill skier
Linda Thom — target shooter
Barbara Underhill and Paul Martini — pairs figure skaters

The People's Choice

CBC televises the first CASBY awards ceremonies. The public chose the Parachute Club as last year's group of the year, and their *At the Feet of the Moon* has won album of the year. The Spoons' "Tell No Lies" was picked as the best single, Bruce Cockburn was best male vocalist, and Jane Siberry was best female vocalist. Luba and Gowan were chosen the most promising female and male artists, and U-2 won best international album of the year. Carole Pope and Paul Shaffer hosted the show, which came complete with a congratulatory message from Prime Minister Mulroney.

Trivia tidbit
Each year National Wildlife Week is held the week of April 10 in honour of Canadian naturalist Jack Miner, who was born on that day.

What's *that?!?*   Hot spring
Banff, Alberta, is famous around the world for its hot springs. A hot spring is a natural flow of water that has worked its way up from the semi-molten layer of the earth's crust. Some people think bathing in its waters is therapeutic.

Did you know?
There's lots of folklore surrounding predictions of rain. Some people say you can tell that April showers are coming by checking your fiddle or violin. If it won't stay in tune, rain isn't far away. Low-flying swallows also indicate rain, as do those red skies in the morning.

APRIL

Monday
1
April Fool's Day
Students at Newtonbrook High in Toronto put their school
— "a 106-room mansion on 5 1/2 acres of well-kept grounds
in the heart of Willowdale" — up for sale in the classifieds.

Tuesday
2
The Cincinnati Reds win on the baseball diamond. As of today's exhibition
game against the Minnesota Twins, Pete Rose is batting a mean 800.
☆ 1940 — birth of Donald Jackson, Olympic figure skater

Wednesday
3
Cyndi Lauper's "Time after Time" wins in six categories at the
third annual American Video Awards. Weird Al Yankovic wins
for "Eat It," his take-off on Michael Jackson's "Beat It."
☆ 1918 — birth of Louis Applebaum, composer and conductor

Thursday
4
Before beginning Bach's "Goldberg Variations" at Edmonton's Jubilee
Auditorium, pianist Rosalyn Tureck takes out her handkerchief and dusts the
piano keys. Then she gives what critics are calling a perfect performance.
☆ 1940 — birth of Phoebe Gilman, author-illustrator of the Jillian Jiggs books

Friday
5
Passover
More than 5000 radio stations around the world, including 400 in Canada,
broadcast "We Are the World" simultaneously to raise more
money for African famine relief.
☆ 1920 — birth of Arthur Hailey, writer

Saturday
6
They're being called the Great Drain Robbers. After a weekend
of tunnelling into a Dublin bank, would-be thieves end up in
the women's washroom. As the alarms go off, they flee without a penny.

Sunday
7
Easter
In California, passenger Michael Lewis asks where to catch the flight from Los
Angeles to Oakland, about 600 km away. He goes where he's told and ends up
on a flight to Auckland, New Zealand, nearly 12 000 km away!
☆ 1908 — birth of Percy Faith, composer-arranger

Monday
8
Someone spots Steve Farkas wiping the lock after storing
something in a locker at the Hamilton, Ontario, bus terminal.
Police are called and, suspecting a bomb, set off a "bomb" of
their own to destroy what's inside. Bye, bye Farkas's prized violin.
☆ 1906 — birth of Raoul Jobin, internationally renowned tenor

Tuesday
9
It's Day Three of National Wildlife Week, a great day to check out an exhibition
of wildlife art by Glen Loates at the Royal Ontario Museum in Toronto.
☆ 1893 — birth of Mary Pickford, actor and co-founder of United Artists

Wednesday
10
Singer Anne Murray and jazz pianist Oscar Peterson
are named Companions to the Order of Canada.
☆ 1865 — birth of John Thomas "Jack" Miner,
conservationist

APRIL

Thursday 11

Thirteen-year-old Joanna Luft touches all the legal bases and finally wins the right to play for a Kitchener Minor Baseball Association all-boys team.
☆ **1914** — birth of Norman McLaren, animated-film maker

Friday 12

The space shuttle *Discovery* lifts off from Cape Canaveral carrying a Canadian 16-channel Anik C satellite that will be launched into orbit during this trip in space.

Saturday 13

The team of 400 water bombers, including two Canadians, fighting the Galapagos island fire can take a break. They flew 150 missions in the past week to bring the fire under control. At last the turtles and flamingos are safe.
☆ **1861** — birth of Margaret Marshall Saunders, author of *Beautiful Joe*

Sunday 14

Fifty-four talented artists and writers, including Stephen King, are producing an "X-Men" comic to raise funds for the Ethiopian relief effort.
☆ **1918** — birth of Scott Young, journalist and author of *A Boy at the Leafs' Camp*

Monday 15

Heart transplant recipient Brian Price of Britain completes the Boston Marathon in 5 hours, 57 minutes and 49 seconds. Toronto's Dr. Terry Kavanagh and his rehabilitation team supervised Price's run.
☆ **1841** — birth of Joseph Emm Seagram, distiller and champion horse breeder

Tuesday 16

Shuttle astronauts use the Canadarm to try to rescue a satellite that's adrift. They also take a two-hour walk in space.
☆ **1949** — birth of Sandy Hawley, jockey

Wednesday 17

Wildlife officials are giving up the search for monsters in Saddle Lake, Alberta. Local residents have reported more than 100 sightings of a serpent-like creature in the past ten years.
☆ **1949** — birth of Martyn Godfrey, author of *Mall Rats*

Thursday 18

Canadian Olympic boxer Shawn O'Sullivan wins a unanimous decision over Dexter Smith of Florida. O'Sullivan has won all four matches he's fought since he turned pro.
☆ **1953** — birth of Rick Moranis, comedian and actor

Friday 19

Toronto's CITY-TV makes final preparations to launch its newest show — *Fashion Television*, with Jeanne Beker as host.
☆ **1900** — birth of Daniel Roland Michener, former governor general of Canada

Saturday 20

About 100 sympathizers gather on Parliament Hill to celebrate the second anniversary of the peace camp set up to protest against cruise missile testing in Canada. The camp itself is down to three people and one tent now.
☆ **1949** — birth of Toller Cranston, figure skater and artist

APRIL

Sunday 21

Lindsay Eberhardt of Malton, Ontario, who received a liver transplant as a baby, celebrates her third birthday on the eve of National Organ Donor Awareness Week.
☆ **1841** — birth of Jennie Kidd Trout, first woman licensed to practise medicine in Canada

Monday 22

Earth Day
The makers of *Toby McTeague*, a Canadian movie being shot in Quebec, need snow, but have had to order 320 kg of instant mashed potatoes instead. The fake flakes are biodegradable, and birds love them too.
☆ **1952** — birth of Kathy Stinson, author of *The Fabulous Ball Book*

Tuesday 23

Coke drinkers are stunned to hear that the 99-year-old recipe for their favourite brew will be changed. The switchboard at Coca-Cola's Atlanta headquarters lights up with thousands of callers objecting to the change.
☆ **1897** — birth of Lester Pearson, 14th prime minister of Canada

Wednesday 24

The CASBY music awards are launched. Nova Scotian Annette Mutsaers wins $1000 for the name, an acronym for Canadian Artists Selected By You.

Thursday 25

Nova Scotia premier John Buchanan's daughter joins a student march on the Legislature to protest against government cutbacks to education spending. What will Dad say when he gets home?

Friday 26

Canada's Rhinoceros Party disbands a few days after its founder, Dr. Jacques Ferron, dies. Dr. Ferron and a few friends formed the party in 1963 to inject a little humour into federal election campaigns.
☆ **1948** — birth of Alfred Sung, fashion designer

Saturday 27

Some kids visiting a library in Hamburg, West Germany, find more than reading material. They discover a 1.5-m python! No one knows how the snake got there.
☆ **1948** — birth of Michael Arvaarluk Kusugak, author of *Northern Lights: The Soccer Trails*

Sunday 28

Sabino Juarez is this year's three-millionth visitor to Disneyland. He wins a shiny new Cadillac.
☆ **1935** — birth of Robert "Bob" White, labour leader

Monday 29

Sylvester Stallone phones Steve Fonyo to tell him that his determination during the Journey for Lives cross-Canada run will inspire him when he's doing the fight scenes in *Rocky IV*.

Tuesday 30

René Jalbert is one of 15 Americans and Canadians to receive a Carnegie Medal for heroism. Jalbert is the Sergeant-at-Arms who spent four hours negotiating with a gunman in the Quebec National Assembly last May.
☆ **1951** — birth of Ken Whiteley, musician and children's recording artist

Extra! Extra!

Folk Flock to Folk Art

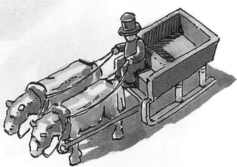

The Royal Ontario Museum is the final stop for a two-year cross-country travelling exhibition of Canadian folk art called *From the Heart*. The art show has delighted thousands of Canadians with displays of handmade items similar to those they may have in their own homes. Visitors to the ROM show will see things such as handcarved toys, exotic bird houses, delicate calligraphy, wild and crazy lawn ornaments, traditional paintings and multicoloured quilts.

Well Done, Steve!

There were many times over the last 14 months when one-legged runner Steve Fonyo wanted to pack it all in. His artificial leg caused him a lot of pain, people didn't know about the run for the first few months, and crossing the Prairies in winter was pretty cold. But Fonyo isn't a quitter. He lost his leg to bone cancer when he was only 12. At 15, he was inspired by Terry Fox's cross-country run, and last year he took on the same challenge in the hope of raising still more money for cancer research.

Trivia tidbit

A new running shoe plugs into your home computer to tell you how far you ran and how many calories you burned up.

Did you know?

Table tennis's other name — Ping-Pong — comes from the sound the ball makes when it bounces off the paddle and the table. The first paddles were made of parchment stretched around a wooden frame.

What's *that?!?* Tornado

Tornado probably comes from the Spanish word for thunderstorm — *tronada*. A tornado is a fast-spinning column of air that looks like a dark, funnel-shaped cloud. The air pressure inside the funnel is so low that objects right underneath it can be sucked up in the same way that dirt is sucked into a vacuum-cleaner hose.

MAY

Wednesday 1

Six Canadians are among the 40 musicians chosen to play in the 1985 international Bach piano competition being held in Toronto this week.
☆ 1831 — birth of Emily Stowe, first Canadian woman to practise medicine in Canada

Thursday 2

Forty-two years of Conservative rule in Ontario will soon be over, as voters elect a minority Conservative government.
☆ 1925 — birth of John Neville, actor and theatre director

Friday 3

Team Canada finishes second in this year's Canada Cup series. Team Czechoslovakia wins gold.
☆ 1913 — birth of Joyce Barkhouse, author of *Pit Pony*

Saturday 4

Betty Kennedy, journalist and *Front Page Challenge* panelist for the past 21 years, and Montreal cartoonist Terry Mosher are among those inducted into the Canadian News Hall of Fame.
☆ 1918 — birth of Lyn Cook, author of *The Hiding Place*

Sunday 5

Shortly after celebrating their second anniversary in April, the Parliament Hill peace campers are evicted from the hill. They had been protesting against cruise missile testing.
☆ 1843 — birth of William Beers, lacrosse player and supporter

Monday 6

The group Alabama is the biggest winner ever in the 20-year history of the Academy of Country Music Awards. It won entertainer of the year, vocal group of the year and album of the year.

Tuesday 7

Number one on the movie video rental list in Toronto this past week was *The Terminator*. *The Pope of Greenwich Village* was second and *Supergirl* was third.
☆ 1937 — birth of Claude Raymond, baseball player and sports commentator

Wednesday 8

Ken Taylor, Canadian ambassador to the United States, receives the Harry S. Truman Good Neighbor Award for his efforts to keep six American hostages safe in Iran six years ago.

Thursday 9

Peace groups lose a court fight to try to stop cruise missile testing in Canada.
☆ 1962 — birth of Shawn O'Sullivan, Olympic boxer

Friday 10

Coca-Cola's latest beverage, New Coke, has arrived!
☆ 1958 — birth of Gaëtan Boucher, Olympic speed skater

Saturday 11

With only one day to go, the Vancouver Children's Festival seems to be a success. Organizers breathe a sigh of relief.
☆ 1943 — birth of Nancy Greene, Olympic alpine skier

MAY

Sunday 12
Mother's Day
A late frost takes its toll on apple and pear trees in British Columbia's Okanagan Valley.
☆ **1921** — birth of Farley Mowat, author of *Lost in the Barrens*

Monday 13
NDP leader Tony Penikett is celebrating his party's upset win in today's territorial elections in the Yukon.
☆ **1937** — birth of Roch Carrier, author of *The Hockey Sweater*

Tuesday 14
The oldest dinosaur skeleton discovered so far has been found in Arizona's Painted Desert. Scientists say the long-necked bird-like creature lived about 225 million years ago.
☆ **1953** — birth of Tom Cochrane, singer-songwriter

Wednesday 15
The USSR declares war on vodka. The drinking age is being raised from 18 to 21, vodka production is being cut back, and liquor can be sold only after 2 P.M. on weekdays.

Thursday 16
A family outing to a national park is going to cost a little more this summer. Parks Canada says entrance fees are going up from $1 to $3 a day.

Friday 17
A two-day Dog Fish Derby begins in British Columbia. Few participants will likely eat their catch, however. Even calling this one-metre-long member of the shark family the salmon shark hasn't improved its public image.
☆ **1898** — birth of A.J. Casson, painter and member of the Group of Seven

Saturday 18
"Motown Returns to the Apollo" is televised tonight to celebrate the Apollo Theatre's reopening and to support Ethiopian famine relief. The star-studded line-up includes Bill Cosby, Stevie Wonder, Little Richard, Joe Cocker and Sammy Davis Jr.
☆ **1963** — birth of Marty McSorley, hockey player

Sunday 19
On the last day of the 13th annual Stage Band Festival in Quebec City, 16-year-old Brad Turner of Langley, British Columbia, is chosen the festival's rising-star trumpet player.
☆ **1817** — birth of Theodore August Heintzman, piano maker

Monday 20
Victoria Day
For the first time in 15 years, the fireworks display at Toronto's Ontario Place is cancelled. Heavy winds and pouring rain are the culprits.
☆ **1929** — birth of Sidney Van den Bergh, astronomer

Tuesday 21
Mariann Domokos of Montreal and Joe Ng of Toronto are the new Canadian table tennis champions following a tournament at York University.
☆ **1887** — birth of James Gladstone (Akay-na-muka), Native senator

MAY

Wednesday 22
A new movie theatre in Vancouver is the first in Canada to get THX — a new sound system nicknamed Lucas Sound because it was developed at the George Lucas studios.

Thursday 23
Seniors begin to organize immediately after Finance Minister Michael Wilson delivers a budget that includes plans to stop increasing old age pensions to match increases in the cost of living.

Friday 24
Pogo the pelican, a resident of England's Chessington Zoo, gets an artificial leg made of fibreglass.
☆ 1902 — birth of Lionel Conacher, all-round athlete

Saturday 25
Student John Kemp is picking up mail from his subdivision's main mailbox in Burlington, Ontario, and delivering it door-to-door to customers for a weekly fee of $1.25. Canada Post won't deliver it, but they don't want him doing it either.
☆ 1858 — birth of James Edward "Tip" O'Neill, record-holding baseball player

Sunday 26
Canadian decathlete Dave Steen finishes fourth at an international meet in East Germany.
☆ 1938 — birth of Teresa Stratas, opera singer

Monday 27
After signing a contract to do a show at the London Palladium in 1996, when he'll be 100, comedian George Burns says he can't afford to die before then because he's already booked.
☆ 1945 — birth of Bruce Cockburn, singer-songwriter

Tuesday 28
New York's Museum of Modern Art proudly receives 72 films by Norman McLaren, Canada's greatest animated-film maker.
☆ 1947 — birth of Lynn Johnston, cartoonist and creator of "For Better or For Worse"

Wednesday 29
In Victoria at last, Steve Fonyo dips his leg in the Pacific Ocean.
☆ 1955 — birth of Michèle Lemieux, illustrator of *There Was an Old Man: A Collection of Limericks*

Thursday 30
The Edmonton Oilers trounce the Philadelphia Flyers in five games to win the Stanley Cup for the second year in a row.

Friday 31
Many Barrie, Ontario, residents are left homeless and businesses are demolished as a tornado slams through the city.
☆ 1961 — birth of Corey Hart, singer-songwriter

JUNE

Extra! Extra!

Keep Out, Stonehenge Visitors Told

On June 21, the nearly 5000-year-old English site of Stonehenge was closed to the public. Officials felt this was the only way to protect the circular monument of stones from damage caused by the large crowds that have gathered there in recent years to celebrate the summer solstice, or longest day. Researchers think Stonehenge was used for ancient religious ceremonies and to observe and measure the movement of the Sun and stars.

The Moon's a Balloon

As of June 15, there's a helium balloon floating over Venus. Suspended from it is one part of a two-part Soviet space probe dropped off near Venus by a spacecraft on its way to take a closer look at Halley's comet. While part one of the probe is taking measurements of the planet's atmosphere, the other part, which released a parachute so it could drift gently to the surface, is busy testing soil samples.

Trivia tidbit

This year nearly 6 million young Canadians are enrolled in elementary and secondary schools.

Did you know?

Venus, the Roman goddess of love after whom the second planet in our solar system is named, was originally the goddess of vegetable gardens.

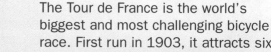

What's *that?!?*   Tour de France

The Tour de France is the world's biggest and most challenging bicycle race. First run in 1903, it attracts six times as many T.V. viewers as the American Super Bowl football game. This year's 4000-km-long route, which includes gruelling rides through the Alps and the Pyrenees, lasts 25 days. Usually, only about half of the starting cyclists make it to the finish line in Paris.

Saturday 1   A Lac St.-Jean marsh has a most welcome weekend visitor — the first white-winged tern ever spotted in Quebec and only the fourth ever seen in Canada.

Sunday 2   Fishing enthusiasts are warned not to eat too many of their catches from the Great Lakes. One fish may contain as many pollutants as a million litres of lake water.

Monday 3   The Boston Celtics' Larry Bird is the National Basketball Association's MVP for the second time in his career.
☆ **1954** — birth of Dan Hill, singer-songwriter

JUNE

Tuesday 4
A truckload of clothing, toys and furniture from concerned Montrealers arrives in Barrie, Ontario, for victims of last month's tornado.
☆ **1951** — birth of Maryann Kovalski, illustrator of *I Went to the Zoo*

Wednesday 5
London's famous clock, Big Ben, is back. For the past two years it was hidden under plastic while being restored to its original glory.
☆ **1939** — birth of Joe Clark, 16th prime minister of Canada

Thursday 6
There's a huge black hole in the middle of the Milky Way. Berkeley, California, scientists say the collapsed star has 4 million times the mass of the Sun.
☆ **1942** — birth of Jan Andrews, author of *The Auction*

Friday 7
Rumour has it that today is Goof-Off Day, so about 2000 Toronto high school students take an unscheduled "field trip" to the Toronto Islands beaches.
☆ **1929** — birth of John Turner, 17th prime minister of Canada

Saturday 8
Bargain hunter Henry Fowlds snaps up 20 umbrellas for $55 at the annual auction of unclaimed items left on Toronto's buses and subway cars. Other items up for grabs: 10-speed bicycles, a computer monitor and an electric guitar.
☆ **1905** — birth of Ralph Steinhauer, first Native Canadian lieutenant governor

Sunday 9
Series MVP Kareem Abdul-Jabbar leads the Los Angeles Lakers to the NBA championship. The Lakers win 111–110 in the sixth and final game.
☆ **1961** — birth of Michael J. Fox, actor

Monday 10
Christopher, Jennifer, Michael and Ashley top the list of parents' choices of children's names, with Matthew, David, Amanda and Sarah not far behind.

Tuesday 11
Canadian rocker Nash the Slash is suing Pepsi-Cola Canada for using a look-alike, complete with shades and a bandaged head, in a T.V. ad.

Wednesday 12
Pittsburg Penguin Mario Lemieux is this year's NHL rookie-of-the-year.
☆ **1959** — birth of Steve Bauer, Olympic cyclist

Thursday 13
The Supreme Court rules that many of Manitoba's laws aren't valid unless they are translated into French.
☆ **1924** — birth of Harold Town, artist

Friday 14
A parliamentary committee recommends that Canada replace the dollar bill with an 11-sided, bronze-coated dollar coin slightly bigger than a quarter.

Saturday 15
Calgary's Carolyn Waldo wins gold in solo synchronized swimming at the Rome world championships.
☆ **1789** — birth of Josiah Henson, founder of an Ontario community for fugitive slaves

Sunday 16
Father's Day
It's Grand Prix time at Montreal's Gilles Villeneuve track. Two Ferraris cross the finish line in first and second positions.
☆ **1847** — birth of Arthur Meighen, ninth prime minister of Canada

JUNE

Monday 17
Summer vacation comes two weeks early for about 200 students in Hampden, Newfoundland, when a suspected gas leak leaves the school reeking.
☆ **1930** — birth of Rosemary Brown, politician, writer and social activist

Tuesday 18
Canadian basketball player Bill Wennington is the first-round draft pick of the NBA's Dallas Mavericks.
☆ **1966** — birth of Kurt Browning, Olympic figure skater

Wednesday 19
In Disney's sequel *Return to Oz,* Dorothy is played by Vancouver's Fairuza Balk, 9.
☆ **1902** — birth of Guy Lombardo, musician and conductor

Thursday 20
Statistics Canada says Canadians are working longer days than they were ten years ago. One in eight workers now puts in a 50-hour week.

Friday 21
Summer Solstice
The long-awaited Picasso Exhibition opens at Montreal's Museum of Fine Arts.
☆ **1900** — birth of Edward Samuel Rogers, broadcasting pioneer and inventor

Saturday 22
Toronto Blue Jays T-shirts, pennants, mugs and anything else bearing the team logo are hot sellers in Canadian souvenir shops this summer.

Sunday 23
Saudi Arabia's King Fahd chats with his nephew long, long distance. The Prince Sultan is aboard the space shuttle *Discovery* as the first Arab astronaut.
☆ **1883** — birth of Frederick "Cyclone" Taylor, first star hockey player

Monday 24
Fête Nationale (Quebec)
Mother Teresa of Calcutta is in Toronto to open a new city mission that will be run by members of her religious order.
☆ **1911** — birth of Portia White, world renowned contralto

Tuesday 25
Those attending the annual Canadian Booksellers Association are reminded that one million Canadians can't read.
☆ **1952** — birth of Tololwa Mollel, author of *The King and the Tortoise*

Wednesday 26
Halifax's royal visitor, Prince Andrew, takes the schooner *Bluenose* out for a spin.
☆ **1854** — birth of Sir Robert Borden, eighth prime minister of Canada

Thursday 27
In response to concerned Canadian seniors, the government backs away from plans to de-index old age pensions.

Friday 28
Canada's Steve Bauer is one of the 200 entrants starting the Tour de France cycling race at Vannes, France, today.

Saturday 29
Montreal's Festival International de Jazz gets off to a musical start with a concert headlined by jazz trumpeter Miles Davis.
☆ **1965** — birth of Stephen Fonyo, cross-Canada runner

Sunday 30
To make up for a slight irregularity in the way Earth rotates, one second — called a leap second — is subtracted from official clocks around the world at midnight Greenwich Mean Time.
☆ **1948** — birth of Murray McLauchlan, singer-songwriter

Extra! Extra!

A Record Breaker

The Live Aid concert is staged to raise money for famine-stricken Ethiopia. Carried around the world by satellite, the concert drew the biggest audience in the history of television. Its 1.5 billion viewers more than doubled the number who watched a human's first steps on the moon in 1969.

The Quest for the Cauldron

The Black Cauldron took 12 years to make. Loosely based on a book by Lloyd Alexander, the animated movie cost $25 million to produce. The film is made up of 2.5 million drawings created by more than 60 animators using 1500 L of paint and over 56 km of film stock.

Trivia tidbit

The most commonly misspelled Canadian place name is St. Catharines. It has two *A*s and no apostrophe before the last *S*.

What's *that?!?* Cyclotron

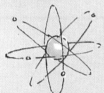

A cyclotron is a scientific tool used to study the physics of the smallest, or sub-atomic, particles of matter. It whips charged particles around in a vacuum, making them go faster and faster on a spiral path, and then lets them fly off in a straight line and smash into a target. Using special detectors, scientists observe the nuclear reactions caused by the collisions.

Did you know?

Tofu, the main ingredient of new frozen desserts, is made from soya beans. The beans are soaked, mashed and strained to extract a thick protein-rich liquid. The protein coagulates to form a curd that's a lot like a soft, white cheese. This bean curd is mixed with other ingredients and flavours, and frozen just like ice cream. Tofu can also be used as a meat substitute.

JULY

Monday
1
Canada Day
Each year on Canada Day the chance of rain in Vancouver is about 23 per cent. In Newfoundland, it's about 57 per cent.
☆ 1952 — birth of Dan Aykroyd, actor

Tuesday
2
It's the oldest known birthday party invitation. Archaeologists have found a letter written nearly 2000 years ago by a Roman woman inviting a friend to her party. The invitation is written in ink on a sliver-thin slice of wood.
☆ 1821 — birth of Sir Charles Tupper, sixth prime minister of Canada

Wednesday
3
CBC announces its fall line-up. Two of the new children's shows scheduled are *Fred Penner's Place* and *Vid Kids*.
The Friendly Giant will be back in re-runs.
☆ 1870 — birth of Richard Bennett, 11th prime minister of Canada

Thursday
4
Giotto, a European space probe, leaves Earth's orbit on a 700-million-km journey. It is scheduled to take a close look at Halley's comet in March of next year.
☆ 1887 — birth of Tom Longboat, long-distance runner

Friday
5
High in the Peruvian Andes, archaeologists are examining the ruins of an ancient terraced city. Hidden under centuries of jungle growth, the city appears to have had as many as 24 000 separate buildings.
☆ 1943 — birth of Robbie Robertson, singer-songwriter

Saturday
6
Hundreds of thousands of fish in a Granby, Quebec, reservoir are dying after workers dumped 40 t of lime into the water yesterday to make it taste and smell better.
☆ 1948 — birth of Lydia Bailey, author of *Vanishing Animals of the Wide Open Spaces*

Sunday
7
The rowing team from Ridley College in St. Catharines, Ontario, wins the Thames Cup final at the famed Henley Royal Regatta in England.

Monday
8
Following his win yesterday, 17-year-old tennis newcomer Boris Becker goes down in the record books as Wimbledon's youngest and first unseeded, or unranked, winner.
☆ 1948 — birth of Raffi (Cavoukian), singer and children's entertainer

Tuesday
9
Scientists from Vancouver's TRIUMPH centre, home to the world's largest cyclotron, are asking for $300 million to build a kaon factory. A kaon is an unstable sub-atomic particle that exists for only one one-hundred-millionth of a second.

Wednesday
10
Deluged by demands for the "old Coke," the soft-drink makers say they'll bring it back under a new name — Coca-Cola Classic.
☆ 1936 — birth of Lois Lilienstein, of Sharon, Lois and Bram

JULY

Thursday 11
Houston Astros' Nolan Ryan strikes out his 4000th batter. That's a new major-league pitching record.
☆ 1950 — birth of Liona Boyd, classical guitarist

Friday 12
How do you spot the tourists at the Calgary Stampede today? They're the ones in fancy cowboy duds. Many of the rodeo cowboys wear safety helmets and running shoes when competing.
☆ 1849 — birth of Sir William Osler, father of modern medicine

Saturday 13
Bob Geldof and Lionel Ritchie offer up the world's biggest rock concert. Fans in more than 150 countries watch the 12-hour-long Live Aid benefit concert broadcast live from London and Philadelphia.
☆ 1934 — birth of Peter Gzowski, journalist, writer and radio celebrity

Sunday 14
Soviet pole vaulter Sergei Bubka has a new world record with a vault of 6.007 m.
☆ 1912 — birth of Northrop Frye, literary critic, professor and writer

Monday 15
Twelve thousand women gather in Nairobi, Kenya, for a conference marking the end of the United Nations Decade for Women.

Tuesday 16
Qing Qing and Quan Quan have arrived. The two giant pandas from China flew into Toronto last night and are settling in for their 100-day stay at the Metro Zoo.

Wednesday 17
A *New England Journal of Medicine* article warns amateurs not to body slam each other the way professional wrestlers do. Apparently, injured fans have been showing up in emergency rooms.
☆ 1935 — birth of Donald Sutherland, actor

Thursday 18
The Yukon becomes the last region in Canada to ban drinking and driving.
☆ 1911 — birth of Hume Cronyn, actor

Friday 19
A $3.5 million tourist centre opens at L'Anse aux Meadows, Newfoundland. The thousand-year-old Viking settlement is the oldest-known European settlement in North America.
☆ 1960 — birth of Atom Egoyan, film maker

Saturday 20
There's a new treat on the market. An Alberta company has come up with Toffait — a frozen dessert made from tofu. It's high in protein, low in calories and fat-free.
☆ 1951 — birth of Paulette Bourgeois, author of the Franklin books

JULY

Sunday
21
France's Bernard Hinault wins his fifth Tour de France. Canada's Steve Bauer finishes in tenth place.
☆ **1926** — birth of Norman Jewison, film director

Monday
22
The killer bees are early. They have shown up in California four years before they were expected to work their way up from Brazil. The good news? Scientists say the colder climate should keep them from travelling too far north.
☆ **1940** — birth of Alex Trebek, host of T.V.'s *Jeopardy*

Tuesday
23
Two Frenchmen, Thierry Caroni and Frederick Beauchene, complete an Atlantic crossing from New York to Falmouth, England. So what? They did it on a windsurfer!

Wednesday
24
The movie *The Black Cauldron* opens in theatres across the country today. It was produced to celebrate Disneyland's 30th anniversary.
☆ **1925** — birth of Gordon "Dr. Zed" Penrose, educator, author and T.V. personality

Thursday
25
The Jeunesses Musicales World Orchestra — 100 international musicians, including 12 from Canada — performs at Notre Dame Basilica in Montreal during the Music of the Americas festival.
☆ **1957** — birth of Steve Podborski, Olympic alpine skier

Friday
26
Toronto's Caribana Festival — a celebration of Caribbean culture — begins today. Parades, picnics, parties and reggae concerts are scheduled throughout the city over the next ten days.
☆ **1943** — birth of Bruce Kidd, runner

Saturday
27
In a record-breaking 11 hours and 47 minutes, Ron Fox and Kevin Jackson of Trenton, Ontario, complete a crossing of Lake Ontario in a racing canoe.
☆ **1934** — birth of James Elder, champion equestrian

Sunday
28
The 25th anniversary Mariposa Folk Festival winds down in Barrie, Ontario. More than 2000 artists have played this gig since it began.
☆ **1958** — birth of Terry Fox, Marathon of Hope runner

Monday
29
People are paying for the privilege of being human billboards. It's becoming more and more difficult to buy a sweatshirt or T-shirt without a company's logo on it.
☆ **1924** — birth of Lloyd Bochner, actor

Tuesday
30
Dene leader Georges Erasmus is elected chief of the Assembly of First Nations.

Wednesday
31
Coleco, makers of the Cabbage Patch doll, announce a new toy — a Rambo doll. They plan on making accessories for it too.

AUGUST

Extra! Extra!

Domed Stadium Gets Green Light

After months of debate, Toronto's City Council has approved plans to build a $150 million domed stadium on the old railway lands beside the CN Tower. The province had approved the project earlier this year, but Torontonians have been worried about how much it will actually cost when it's done. The Blue Jays' new home will have a domed roof that can be left open on sunny days, and can slide closed in less than half an hour.

Once upon a Time ...

There must be a fantasy or fairy-tale bug going around Hollywood this year. The list of films now showing or in the works suggests the theme is contagious. That list includes movies such as *Back to the Future*, *Lady Hawke*, *Labyrinth*, *The Black Cauldron*, *Legend*, *The Princess Bride*, *Highlander*, *Return to Oz* and *Peter Pan*.

Trivia tidbit

Scientifically, a month is the time it takes the Moon to make one full trip around Earth — 29 days, 12 hours, 44 minutes and 2.8 seconds.

What's *that?!?*   *Surimi*

Invented in Japan, *surimi* is a fish paste made from cleaned, deboned and washed fresh fillets. The fillets are mixed with natural crab flavours and a few other ingredients, and are processed to make them look and taste like pieces of crab meat.

Did you know?

The serum used to de-sensitize people seriously allergic to bee and wasp stings is made from the insects' venom or poison. Sensitive people are regularly injected with small amounts of the serum to make their bodies produce antibodies that will combat the venom.

AUGUST

Thursday 1
Doctors are advising people who react strongly to insect bites to keep emergency sting kits handy in the summer. These kits contain single doses of a drug called epinephrine, which can prevent allergic shock.
☆ **1942** — birth of Michael Martchenko, illustrator of *Where There's Smoke*

Friday 2
Nearly 10 000 campers from the Maritimes, Louisiana, and St. Pierre and Miquelon are gathered at Cape St. George, Newfoundland, for the start of Une Longue Veillée, a French folk festival.
☆ **1942** — birth of André Gagnon, pianist and composer

Saturday 3
Tommy Hunter, Jerry Lee Lewis, Tammy Wynette and Wilf Carter are just a few of the folk in town for the Brooks, Alberta, Rocky Mountain Country Jamboree.

Sunday 4
Canadian driver Jacques Villeneuve beats out Michael Andretti to win his first Indy car race at Elkhart Lake, Wisconsin.
☆ **1921** — birth of Maurice "Rocket" Richard, hockey player

Monday 5
Civic Holiday
Makers of *Back to the Future* have refunded $25 000 to the California Raisin Board because a scene the board had paid for — showing Michael J. Fox eating raisins — was cut from the movie.
☆ **1948** — birth of Sue Hammond, creator of *Beethoven Lives Upstairs*

Tuesday 6
Hiroshima Day
Chris Heads, 11, pulls his two buddies from the grip of arctic wolves at the Metro Toronto Zoo. The three boys had sneaked into an area that is off-limits to the public.

Wednesday 7
A new computerized system will keep track of the more than 12 000-a-day personal long-distance calls federal workers make at taxpayers' expense.
☆ **1965** — birth of Elizabeth Manley, Olympic figure skater

Thursday 8
Baseball players are back in the game after being on strike for three days.
☆ **1949** — birth of Patti Stren, author of *I Was a 15-Year-Old Blimp*

Friday 9
Nagasaki commemorates the 40th anniversary of the bombing of this city by releasing 500 white peace doves.
☆ **1964** — birth of Brett Hull, hockey player

Saturday 10
Newfoundland's Terra Nova Fishery Co. has a supermarket hit. It's Canadian-made *surimi*, a processed seafood product that looks and tastes like crab but costs a lot less.
☆ **1959** — birth of Florent Vollant, of the musical group Kashtin

AUGUST

Sunday 11
An American icebreaker completes a voyage through Canadian Arctic waters without first asking Canada. The trip is seen as a challenge to Canada's claims to the Northwest Passage territories.

Monday 12
David Frank of Toronto ends a record-breaking 36 hours, 43 minutes and 40 seconds of skateboarding. He covered 432.77 km during his marathon effort.
☆ **1949** — birth of Christiane Duchesne, author of *Victor*

Tuesday 13
Just three days after receiving a new heart, Calgarian Dale Robinson says he feels ready to get up and go for a walk. The nurses won't let him do that just yet.
☆ **1949** — birth of Bobby Clarke, hockey player

Wednesday 14
School boards across the country scramble to find new teachers for the increasing number of students enrolling in French immersion programs.
☆ **1962** — birth of Horst Bulau, ski jumper

Thursday 15
Just 165 km from the coast and from a new record for an Atlantic crossing, Richard Branson's powerboat flips over and sinks. He's safe, but sorry.
☆ **1925** — birth of Oscar Peterson, jazz pianist

Friday 16
Cheering Kenyans welcome Pope John Paul II on his first visit to Nairobi.
☆ **1940** — birth of Linda Manning, author of *Dinosaur Days*

Saturday 17
One of the troops is AWOL — absent without official leave — from Canadian Forces Base Trenton. He's a three-month-old falcon used to scare other birds away from the base's runways.
☆ **1964** — birth of Colin James, singer-songwriter

Sunday 18
Michael Jackson pays $40 million for the rights to nearly 5000 songs, including most of those written by Beatles John Lennon and Paul McCartney.
☆ **1906** — birth of Arthur LeBlanc, musician known as "the Acadian poet of the violin"

Monday 19
Canada Council awards are presented in Montreal. For children's literature, Marie-Louise Gay wins two — for *Lizzy's Lion* (illustrator) and *Drôle d'école* (author). Jan Hudson's *Sweetgrass* and Daniel Sernine's *Le Cercle Violet* win too.

Tuesday 20
In Banff, Prince Philip unveils a plaque declaring the national park a UNESCO World Heritage Site.
☆ **1957** — birth of Cindy Nicholas, marathon swimmer

Wednesday 21
Montreal's ninth annual World Film Festival starts today, with more than 60 countries represented.

AUGUST

Thursday 22
Archaeologists worry that the Mackenzie River is slowly washing away artifacts of early Inuit settlements along the river's shores.
☆ **1943** — birth of Vlasta van Kampen, illustrator of *King of Cats*

Friday 23
In an effort to escape, two prisoners crawl for hours through the ventilation system of Quebec Provincial Police headquarters. They end up right above the guards' lunchroom.
☆ **1959** — birth of Nino Ricci, author

Saturday 24
Players from Seoul, South Korea, are the proud winners of the 39th annual Little League World Series, held this year in Williamsport, Pennsylvania.
☆ **1922** — birth of René Lévesque, Quebec politician and journalist

Sunday 25
Three Dutch balloonists take off from St. John's, Newfoundland, in search of a new record for crossing the Atlantic in a hot-air balloon.

Monday 26
Three Dutch balloonists and their downed craft, the Flying Dutchman, are plucked from the Atlantic about 870 nautical miles off the coast of Ireland.
☆ **1957** — birth of Rick Hansen, wheelchair athlete

Tuesday 27
After three weeks as the No. 1 single on the North American charts, "Shout," by Tears for Fears, has to make way for "The Power of Love," by Huey Lewis and the News.

Wednesday 28
Martina Navratilova makes money just getting dressed these days. Advertisers pay her more than $2 million a year to wear their shoes, their tops, their headbands and anything else the television cameras might pick up.
☆ **1926** — birth of Ted Harrison, author-illustrator of *O Canada*

Thursday 29
More than half a million people have visited the giant pandas who've taken up temporary residence at Toronto's zoo. A share of ticket and souvenir sales will go to the China Wildlife Association.

Friday 30
Terry David Mulligan, popular host of CBC Vancouver's *Good Rockin' Tonight,* announces that he's leaving the show to become MuchMusic's west coast correspondent.
☆ **1933** — birth of Don Getty, Alberta politician

Saturday 31
Musique Plus, the French equivalent of MuchMusic, takes to the airwaves.
☆ **1903** — birth of Helen Irene Battle, pioneering woman zoologist

SEPTEMBER

Extra! Extra!

Canada from *A* to *Z*

Edmonton publisher Mel Hurtig can finally relax. After six years of hard work, his baby — the first new Canadian encyclopedia since 1958 — has arrived at last. The three-volume encyclopedia contains 8000 entries and 3.2 million words. Nearly 5000 people worked to complete the project.

Symbolic Birds

In September, Manitoba became the ninth region of Canada to name an official bird. Eight other regions already have an official feathered friend.

Alberta — great horned owl
British Columbia — Stellar's jay
New Brunswick — black-capped chickadee
Ontario — common loon
Prince Edward Island — blue jay
Quebec — snowy owl
Saskatchewan — sharp-tailed grouse
Yukon — common raven

Trivia tidbit

In 1985, Ontario hens laid 194 803 000 dozen eggs. That's more than 2 billion 300 million eggs!

What's *that?!?* Triskaidekaphobe

Triskaidekaphobes have an irrational fear or phobia about the number 13, believing it to be very unlucky. Some people also believe that Fridays are unlucky days, so Friday the 13th packs a double whammy for superstitious people.

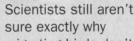

Did you know?

Scientists still aren't sure exactly why migrating birds don't get lost. They do know that the changing length of day is the signal for them to begin their journey south or north. They also know that you can use artificial light to confuse birds temporarily about what time of day it is, or which direction is which. Attaching small magnets to their bodies leaves birds much more confused. This suggests that they use Earth's magnetic field as well as the Sun as a direction finder.

Sunday
1
Space shuttle *Discovery* astronauts accidentally launched a screwdriver into orbit today while working to release three communications satellites.
☆ **1926** — birth of James Reaney, poet and writer

Monday
2
Labour Day
Researchers using a remote-controlled submarine called *Argo* announce that they have located the wreckage of the *Titanic* 4 km under water about 800 km southeast of Newfoundland.

Tuesday
3
Vancouver's Bryan Adams and Montreal's Corey Hart each get Juno nominations in the same four categories.
☆ **1893** — birth of Norma Ford Walker, geneticist

SEPTEMBER

Wednesday
4

Lincoln Alexander, Ontario's new lieutenant governor, is the first black person to hold the vice-regal post in Canada.

Thursday
5

A Scarborough, Ontario, supermarket is Canada's first with a computerized shelf display. Shoppers push a button, and a small electronic display on the shelf shows the item's price, unit cost and savings to be had if it's on sale.
☆ 1916 — birth of Frank Shuster, comedian of "Wayne and Shuster" fame

Friday
6

The Canadian Encyclopedia hits the bookstores, and first-day sales across the country are brisk.

Saturday
7

First-year students at the University of Toronto kidnap the Festival of Festival's blimp as it floats over Toronto's Park Plaza Hotel.

Sunday
8

Baseball's Pete Rose ties Ty Cobb's career record of 4191 hits set back in 1928.
☆ 1937 — birth of Barbara Frum, broadcast journalist

Monday
9

The Loch Ness monster? No, just a World War II bomber that was ditched in the famous lake 35 years ago. A salvage company has begun pulling it out.

Tuesday
10

The Germazian brothers open phase three of their West Edmonton Mall. The mall is now 1.6 km long, bigger than 80 football fields, and home to 825 stores.
☆ 1907 — birth of Fay Wray, actor

Wednesday
11

Jean Howarth reports that her family's pet raccoon, Robber, is guarding their orchard by pitching apples at raiding wild raccoons.

Thursday
12

Members of the South African government recommend that the country's racist pass laws be abolished. The pass laws prevent people of colour from going to certain places at certain times.
☆ 1937 — birth of George Chuvalo, champion heavyweight boxer

Friday
13

France's President Mitterrand's Concorde jet breaks down twice before it finally takes off for French Guiana. Then, just nine minutes after it is launched, the Ariana rocket he has come to see explodes. Triskaidekaphobes aren't surprised.
☆ 1775 — birth of Laura Secord, War of 1812 heroine

Saturday
14

In St. John's, Newfoundland, Canada's soccer team beats Honduras to earn its first-ever appearance in a World Cup playoff. Mexico, here we come!
☆ 1940 — birth of Barbara Greenwood, author of *A Pioneer Story*

Sunday
15

Rosh Hashanah
Hundreds of thousands of Canadians at home and abroad take part in the fifth annual Terry Fox run to raise funds for cancer research.

Monday
16

Canada launches its Olympic coin series. The collectors items are expected to raise up to $60 million to help pay for the Calgary Winter Olympics in 1988.
☆ 1926 — birth of Takao Tanabe, artist

Tuesday
17

Soviet cosmonauts Alexander Volkov and Georgy Grechko arrive at the Salyut 7 space station, replacing a cosmonaut who has been aboard since June.

SEPTEMBER

Wednesday
18
Canadians are checking their cupboards after learning that a million cans of rancid tuna have been sold over the past several months.
☆ 1895 — birth of John Diefenbaker, 13th prime minister of Canada

Thursday
19
A massive earthquake measuring 7.3 on the Richter scale causes extensive damage in Mexico City.
☆ 1951 — birth of Daniel Lanois, singer, composer and record producer

Friday
20
Apple Canada announces it is bringing out Apple II and Macintosh computers with colour monitors and 3 1/2-inch disk drives.
☆ 1951 — birth of Guy Lafleur, hockey player

Saturday
21
An in-transit bald eagle wows visitors at a Lake Erie lookout east of Port Stanley, Ontario. He's going south, but where he's coming from is a mystery.
☆ 1934 — birth of Leonard Cohen, poet and singer-songwriter

Sunday
22
Tonight, "Farm Aid" is on T.V. The benefit concert to help farmers plagued by bad weather, dropping prices and overdue bank loans features such stars as Willie Nelson, Neil Young and Kenny Rogers.

Monday
23
Autumn Equinox
Growing Pains, starring Canadian actor-writer-producer Alan Thicke, debuts on T.V.
☆ 1946 — birth of Anne Wheeler, film maker

Tuesday
24
Jason Bunn of Leeds, England, wins the World Monopoly championship held in Atlantic City, New Jersey.

Wednesday
25
Yom Kippur
The doors to the Royal Tyrrell Museum of Palaeontology near Drumheller, Alberta, are officially open to dinosaur fans.
☆ 1943 — birth of Eugenie Fernandes, author-illustrator of *The Tree That Grew to the Moon*

Thursday
26
Hurricane Gloria batters the northeastern United States with driving rain and winds of up to 210 km/h.

Friday
27
Manitobans have chosen the great grey owl as their province's official bird.
☆ 1948 — birth of Mark Thurman, author-illustrator of *One Two Many*

Saturday
28
A Buckingham Palace official says that there's no truth to the rumours about trouble in paradise for Prince Charles and Lady Di.
☆ 1962 — birth of Grant Fuhr, hockey goalie

Sunday
29
Calgary's Peter Butler wins the Toronto Marathon. Butler is also a six-time Canadian champion in the 5000- and 10 000-km events.
☆ 1946 — birth of Allen Morgan, author of *Ryan's Giant*

Monday
30
Canada's wrestling squad wins every one of its 14 matches today at the Commonwealth championships being held in Glasgow, Scotland.
☆ 1940 — birth of Harry Jerome, world champion sprinter

OCTOBER

Extra! Extra!

Trouble in Pumpkin Heaven

Michael Hodgson has won the $3000 prize at the International Pumpkin Festival, but the festival itself has competition. The newcomer, the World Pumpkin Federation, won't recognize winning weights in the International contest and has picked its own world champ — Connecticut's Scott Cully, who grew a smaller pumpkin.

Top Albums of 1985

♪ *Born in the USA*, Bruce Springsteen
♪ *Like a Virgin*, Madonna
♪ *No Jacket Required*, Phil Collins
♪ *Make It Big*, Wham!
♪ *We Are the World*, USA for Africa

Trivia tidbit
In 1985, the minimum wage for full-time workers in Canada ranged from $3.65 in British Columbia to $4.50 in Saskatchewan.

Did you know?
A celebration of some sort goes on somewhere in the world on each of the "quarter days" of the year, those days that mark the halfway points between the equinoxes and the solstices: February 2 (Groundhog Day), May 1 (May Day), August 1 (Lammas Day) and October 31 (Hallowe'en).

What's *that?!?*   Panda
Scientists have often argued over what type of animal a panda is. Some have said that it's not really a bear, but belongs in the same group as raccoons. Others say it's much more like a bear than anything else. Still others say it's such an unusual creature, it belongs in a class of its own.

OCTOBER

Tuesday
1
A tiny North American warbler is spotted in southern England. Hurricane Gloria seems to have blown it 3000 nautical miles off its migrating route to Brazil.
☆ **1926** — birth of Ben Wicks, cartoonist

Wednesday
2
As of yesterday, Canada's official population is 25 444 900.

Thursday
3
Sales of Swiss-made Swatch watches continue to soar in Canada and the United States this year, and are predicted to reach the 3.5-million mark by Christmas.
☆ **1882** — birth of Alexander Young "A.Y." Jackson, painter and member of the Group of Seven

Friday
4
University of Chicago chemists suggest that dinosaurs may have died from breathing soot-filled air caused by a huge fire.
☆ **1934** — birth of Rudy Wiebe, author

Saturday
5
Ontario stuntman David Manley finally makes his boyhood dream come true. He goes over Niagara Falls in a barrel complete with a video camera to catch the action.
☆ **1965** — birth of Mario Lemieux and Patrick Roy, hockey players

Sunday
6
Residents of Fort Simpson, Northwest Territories, learn that yesterday's earthquake was a 6.6 on the Richter scale. Fortunately, the epicentre was far enough away from all populated areas that there was little damage.
☆ **1866** — birth of Reginald Aubrey Fessenden, inventor of the radio

Monday
7
In Toronto, comedian Andrea Martin hosts a fund-raising fashion show of Canadian designs to raise money for Canadian Physicians for African Relief.

Tuesday
8
Freedom to Read Week begins across Canada. This year's focus is on the effects of censorship on schools and libraries.

Wednesday
9
Construction of Vancouver's new elevated rapid transit system is right on schedule. It's a 23-km-long people-mover being built for next year's World's Fair at a cost of about $1 billion.
☆ **1967** — birth of Carling Bassett, tennis player

Thursday
10
In a special ceremony, Strawberry Fields, a new peace garden in New York's Central Park, is dedicated to the memory of John Lennon.
☆ **1863** — birth of Louis Cyr, strongman

Friday
11
A million recalled tins of tainted tuna may soon be back on supermarket shelves — as pet food, not people food this time.
☆ **1933** — birth of Walter Babiak, musician-conductor for Classical Kids' recordings

OCTOBER

Saturday 12
Famous Players theatres are doing something new — showing videos before the main feature. The video currently playing is Live Aid's "Dancing in the Streets."
☆ **1880** — birth of Healey Willan, composer

Sunday 13
Physicists at Fermilab, in Illinois, switch on the world's largest particle accelerator, or atom smasher.
☆ **1955** — birth of Jane Siberry, singer-songwriter

Monday 14
Thanksgiving
Qing Qing and Quan Quan, pandas visiting the Metro Toronto Zoo, receive their millionth visitor today.
☆ **1927** — birth of Elmer Isler, choir conductor

Tuesday 15
Nova Scotia's Michael Hodgson loves his world championship pumpkin — a 241-kg, bright orange beauty.
☆ **1908** — birth of John Kenneth Galbraith, economist

Wednesday 16
The Blue Jays miss out on the American League pennant, losing 6–2 to the Kansas City Royals.

Thursday 17
Wrinkles, the Puppet is the winner of the Canadian Toy Testing Council's first Toy of the Year award. The floppy-eared hound is another bestseller for Ganz Bros. Toys in Woodbridge, Ontario.
☆ **1948** — birth of Margot Kidder, actor

Friday 18
The sixth annual International Festival of Authors opens in Toronto. More than 45 authors and poets from around the world will give readings in the next eight days.
☆ **1919** — birth of Pierre Elliott Trudeau, 15th prime minister of Canada .

Saturday 19
Toronto kicks off its Week of the Child with a lively concert starring Sandra Beech, Chris Whitely, Bill Russell and Caitlin Hanford.

Sunday 20
After a wet summer, grasshoppers and early snow, Manitoba farmers take advantage of the weekend's unusually warm weather to harvest as much of their surviving crops as they can.
☆ **1945** — birth of Jo Ellen Bogart, author of *Gifts*

Monday 21
More than 10 000 striking Chrysler Canada workers are starting to return to work after six days on the picket line.

Tuesday 22
Game 18 of the world championship re-match chess match between Karpov and Kasparov ends in a draw. There's a 24-game limit to this match.
☆ **1844** — birth of Louis Riel, Métis leader

October

Wednesday 23

A report from the Science Council of Canada recommends that the government set up a Canadian Space Agency to plan for this country's future role in space exploration and satellite communications.
☆ **1963** — birth of Gordon Korman, author of *Why Did the Underwear Cross the Road?*

Thursday 24

Peace marches, ceremonies and services are held to mark the designation by the United Nations of next year as the International Year of Peace.

Friday 25

Canadians frustrated with the fitness craze and workout videos can buy a new release called *Pig Out* by a hefty truck driver named Hughie Hubert. People are walking, not running, to buy it, but sales are good.
☆ **1966** — birth of Wendel Clark, hockey player

Saturday 26

In a highly symbolic ceremony, the Australian government returns Ayers Rock to its rightful owners, the Aborigines.

Sunday 27

The Kansas City Royals defeat the St. Louis Cardinals to win the World Series.
☆ **1928** — birth of Gilles Vigneault, singer-songwriter and poet

Monday 28

Céline Dion takes home five of the Quebec music industry's ADISQ awards, including female singer of the year. Corey Hart wins in the male category.

Tuesday 29

Canadian figure skaters Isabelle and Paul Duchesnay are moving to France, where they also hold citizenship, to compete for a place on that country's skating team.
☆ **1959** — birth of Mike Gartner, hockey player

Wednesday 30

More than 700 students at a St. Stephen, New Brunswick, high school eat 1200 tuna sandwiches for lunch to show support for laid-off workers at the local tuna packing plant.
☆ **1953** — birth of Robin Muller, author-illustrator of *Little Wonder*

Thursday 31

Hallowe'en
The Sailcats, a Calgary-based rock band, beat out 632 other groups to win the Music Express–MuchMusic National Talent Search contest.
☆ **1950** — birth of John Candy, comedian and actor

Extra! Extra!

Humphrey Is Free

Humphrey is a 12-m-long whale who wandered into San Francisco in October and has spent three weeks swimming nearly 120 km upriver to check out the scenery. People tried to shoo him back to the sea, but he ignored all their efforts. Finally he made up his own mind, turned around and made a bee-line for home. Hundreds of boats cheered him on as he swam under the Golden Gate Bridge and back out to sea.

15th Annual Juno Awards

- ♪ Album of the Year — *Reckless*, Bryan Adams
- ♪ Male Vocalist of the Year — Bryan Adams
- ♪ Female Vocalist of the Year — Luba
- ♪ Single of the Year — "Never Surrender," Corey Hart
- ♪ Group of the Year — The Parachute Club

Trivia tidbit

November 1985 proves to be the wettest November for southern Ontario in 145 years. As much as 235 mm of rain fell on some parts of the province.

Did you know?

Comets are small chunks of matter that orbit around the Sun, trailing a stream of gases and dust behind them. When Halley's comet appeared in 1910, hucksters began selling "comet pills" to protect people from the deadly effects of its supposedly poisonous tail.

What's *that?!?* Halley's Comet

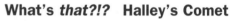

English astronomer Edmond Halley predicted, after years of calculations, that the comet he had seen in 1682 would return in 1758. He asked scientists to watch out for it after he was dead. They did, and he was right. The comet that still comes close to Earth once every 76 years is named after him.

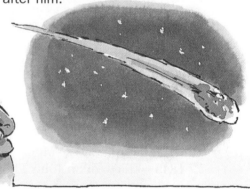

November

Friday 1
Ross Pedler won't lose his pilot's licence after all. He's the flyer who dropped messages and a Canadian flag on an American icebreaker that sailed through the Northwest Passage last summer without Canada's permission.
☆ **1858** — birth of Joseph Burr Tyrrell, geologist and discoverer of Alberta's dinosaur beds

Saturday 2
The soundtrack from the T.V. show *Miami Vice* climbs to No. 1 on the charts.
☆ **1961** — birth of k.d. lang, singer-songwriter

Sunday 3
Overflow crowds line up at a Toronto theatre showing *My American Cousin*, written and directed by Vancouver's Sandy Duncan.
☆ **1925** — birth of Monica Hughes, author of *The Golden Aquarians*

Monday 4
At tonight's Juno Awards, Canadians get to hear k.d. lang, a blues and rockabilly singer who is showing international promise but isn't well known at home.

Tuesday 5
OWL-TV debuts on CBC. The new science and nature program includes *OWL Magazine*'s popular characters Dr. Zed and the Mighty Mites.
☆ **1959** — birth of Bryan Adams, singer-songwriter

Wednesday 6
Protests by a group of Haida bring logging on British Columbia's Queen Charlotte Islands to a halt.
☆ **1945** — birth of Robert Munsch, author of *Wait and See*

Thursday 7
It's the 100th anniversary of the "last spike" ceremony that marked the completion of the Canadian Pacific Railway. Visitors to a railroad exhibition at Victoria's provincial museum can see the second-to-last spike. It bent and had to be replaced.
☆ **1943** — birth of Joni Mitchell, singer-songwriter

Friday 8
A team of Egyptian and American scientists is trying to devise a way to save a precious find in an Egyptian tomb — a sample of 4600-year-old air.
☆ **1940**— birth of Janet Foster, author, naturalist, photographer and film maker

Saturday 9
Canada's Lorne Michaels is back in the director's chair at *Saturday Night Live* to add some oomph to the show.
☆ **1937** — birth of Clyde Wells, Newfoundland politician

Sunday 10
Halley's comet is making its once-every-76-years' appearance. It's now only about 120 675 000 km away from Earth. That's more than 300 times as far away as the Moon.
☆ **1845** — birth of Sir John Thompson, fourth prime minister of Canada

November

Monday 11
Remembrance Day
On a visit to Washington, the Princess of Wales is honoured with a mural of her likeness made out of jellybeans.

Tuesday 12
Denmark's 16-year-old Prince Joachim isn't in class today. He's been suspended for a week for disruptive behaviour during a school play.
☆ **1945** — birth of Neil Young, singer-songwriter

Wednesday 13
Canadian stuntman Steve Trotter strikes again. He climbs down a rope tied to the Golden Gate Bridge with a banner wishing President Reagan good luck at the Soviet Summit. Then he can't get back up. The Coast Guard picks him up and arrests him.

Thursday 14
A volcano erupts in northern Colombia, sending a sea of mud rushing down on towns and villages below.
☆ **1891** — birth of Sir Frederick Banting, co-discoverer of insulin

Friday 15
Fire fighters saw through an ice-covered stream near Thunder Bay to rescue a one-and-a-half-year-old boy who had been trapped under water for 30 minutes.
☆ **1969** — birth of Helen Kelesi, champion tennis player

Saturday 16
The ninth annual national Children's Book Festival opens. This year's theme is the art of the illustrator.
☆ **1947** — birth of Anne Blades, author-illustrator of *Mary of Mile 18*

Sunday 17
Inuit leaders accept an invitation to visit Ethiopia so people there can express their thanks. Per capita, Inuit were the most generous contributors to the Ethiopian famine relief fund. An Inuit leader says his people remember what it's like to starve.
☆ **1946** — birth of Petra Burka, champion figure skater

Monday 18
Police across southern Ontario continue to warn parents and teachers to keep children away from storm sewers, rivers and streams swollen by record rainfalls.
☆ **1939** — birth of Margaret Atwood, author

Tuesday 19
Presidents Gorbachev and Reagan meet for Summit talks in Geneva to discuss arms control. This is the first meeting between Soviet and American leaders in six years.
☆ **1937** — birth of Marilyn Bell, marathon swimmer

Wednesday 20
"The King of Saturday Night," a Canadian video, is a gold-medal winner at the New York Film and Television Festival.
☆ **1841** — birth of Sir Wilfrid Laurier, seventh prime minister of Canada

November

Thursday 21
The Soviets bring back the three remaining cosmonauts from their space lab, Salyut 7, because the commander is sick.
★ **1902** — birth of Foster Hewitt, hockey broadcaster

Friday 22
Prime Minister Brian Mulroney took an extra jet on his Florida vacation last week — just in case the first one broke down.
★ **1950** — birth of Linda Granfield, author of *1988: The Year I Was Born*

Saturday 23
The Thunder Bay toddler rescued more than a week ago from an ice-covered stream is running around as if nothing had happened. He was trapped under water for half an hour.

Sunday 24
The BC Lions beat the Hamilton Tiger Cats 37–14 to finally win the Grey Cup — after a 21-year drought.
★ **1940** — birth of Eric Wilson, author of *The Inuk Mountie*

Monday 25
Today has been designated a special Halley Watch Day. All telescopes are ready and aimed to observe the comet as it makes its closest inbound approach to Earth.

Tuesday 26
A Revenue Canada official says the government spent $50 000 recently on a survey to show that nine out of ten Canadians think of Crest as a toothpaste. No kidding.
★ **1938** — birth of Rich Little, impressionist and comedian

Wednesday 27
Good news. It's warming up in Saskatchewan and Alberta. Yesterday, exposed skin could freeze after just one minute outdoors. Today it takes all of five minutes to get frostbitten.

Thursday 28
Canada has decided what to give the Queen at next year's Commonwealth Games in Edinburgh. She'll be presented with two pesky beavers who kept building dams that flooded a campground in Manitoba's Nopiming Provincial Park. Lucky her.
★ **1851** — birth of Albert Henry George Grey, governor general and donor of football's Grey Cup

Friday 29
A freighter rams into the St. Louis de Gonzaque Bridge, creating a traffic jam of 55 ships trying to get through the St. Lawrence Seaway system before it shuts down for the winter.
★ **1949** — birth of Stan Rogers, singer-songwriter

Saturday 30
Police have identified the car a Soviet freighter hooked when it pulled up anchor in Charlottetown Harbour yesterday. It's a 1975 Buick reported stolen three years ago.
★ **1915** — birth of Henry Taube, Nobel-winning chemist

DECEMBER

Extra! Extra!

Hot Stuff — The Year in Review

Here's a sampling of the people, products and events that dominated the pop scene in 1985:

Live Aid	Boris Becker
Bob Geldof	John Walker
Bryan Adams	Pete Rose
Corey Hart	Manute Bol
Madonna	Reeboks
Michael J. Fox	Gummi Bears
John Candy	Swatches
Dr. Ruth	Tofu
Hulk Hogan	Care Bears

Zapped!

In a spirit of good fun mixed with seriousness, the "Unicorn Hunters" of Lake Superior College have been banishing misused, overused and useless words and phrases from the English language since 1975. This year's list includes *Star Wars*, *busters* (as in "crime busters"), *read* (as in "a good read") and *near miss* (instead of "near hit").

Trivia tidbit

In 1985, Canadian department store sales of toys and games topped the $350 million mark.

What's *that?!?* Payload

On space shuttle flights, the payload is whatever is aboard that helps pay NASA's bills for the shuttle program. For example, other countries and private companies pay to have their satellites launched from the orbiter.

Did you know?

The St. Lawrence Seaway and the Great Lakes Waterway form the largest inland navigation route in North America. The system includes 16 locks that make it possible for boats to "climb" up and down the 174-m elevation difference between Lake Superior and the sea.

Sunday 1 — Nearly five million viewers tune in to part 1 of "Anne of Green Gables," making it the most popular non-sports show in Canadian T.V. history.

Monday 2 — In a Quebec election, the Parti Québécois under Pierre-Marc Johnson is defeated by the Liberals led by Robert Bourassa.

Tuesday 3 — The space shuttle *Atlantis* returns from a seven-day mission during which a payload of three communications satellites were launched.

Wednesday 4 — Health workers from across Canada hold a public forum in Toronto to discuss the rising number of cases of acquired immune deficiency syndrome (AIDS).
☆ 1945 — birth of Roberta Bondar, astronaut, physician and research scientist

December

Thursday 5
Statistics Canada reports that 61 000 households in this country don't have toilets, and more than 90 000 are without bathtubs or showers.
☆ **1914** — birth of Frank Russel Thurston, aircraft engineer

Friday 6
Canada's top-selling band, Platinum Blond, gives a benefit concert in Toronto to raise funds for the United Way.
☆ **1961** — birth of Stephane Poulin, author-illustrator of *Endangered Animals*

Saturday 7
In Rome, 165 Roman Catholic bishops from around the world end a two-week synod, a special meeting to look at changes in the church over the past 20 years.
☆ **1951** — birth of Karen Patkau, author-illustrator of *In the Sea*

Sunday 8
Chanukah begins
Police break up a vigil of about 25 young people braving a Moscow snowstorm to listen to Beatles songs on a portable tape recorder on the fifth anniversary of John Lennon's death.

Monday 9
Bryan Adams receives the Diamond Award for 1 million Canadian sales of his album *Reckless*.

Tuesday 10
Representatives of the International Physicians for the Prevention of Nuclear War are presented with the Nobel Peace Prize.

Wednesday 11
Last year's cookbooks all seemed to be about hors d'oeuvres. This year it's desserts. There's even a recipe for rose-petal ice cream.
☆ **1964** — birth of Carolyn Waldo, Olympic synchronized swimmer

Thursday 12
The Toronto Blizzard soccer team, which folded recently, will become part of a new professional league with teams in Edmonton, Calgary, Vancouver, North York and Hamilton.
☆ **1938** — birth of Mary Blakeslee, author of *Stampede*

Friday 13
After 108 years of using white tennis balls, Wimbledon's tournament organizers have decided to permit the use of easier-to-see yellow balls in next year's matches.
☆ **1929** — birth of Christopher Plummer, actor

Saturday 14
The Canadian Encyclopedia is a popular choice for holiday book buyers this year. There aren't many of the 150 000 sets printed left on the shelves.

Sunday 15
Appearance offers have been pouring in for Quebec mimic André-Philippe Gagnon ever since his recent appearance on Johnny Carson's *Tonight Show*.

Monday 16
"A Young Children's Concert with Raffi" has won the American "Parents' Choice Award" for best children's T.V. show of the year.
☆ **1936** — birth of Karleen Bradford, author of *There Will Be Wolves*

Tuesday 17
A Trent University researcher warns that acid rain is threatening Ontario's loon population.
☆ **1874** — birth of William Lyon Mackenzie King, tenth prime minister of Canada

December

Wednesday 18
Thousands of Filipinos greet presidential candidate Corazon Aquino, who is running against President Ferdinand Marcos in an upcoming election.
☆ **1961** — birth of Brian Orser, Olympic figure skater

Thursday 19
In Paris, Disney officials announce that France has won out over Spain and Portugal in bidding for Europe's first Disneyland theme park.

Friday 20
There's an epidemic of red measles in Vancouver. More than 150 kids are already sick, with others bound to fall ill over the holidays.

Saturday 21
Winter Solstice
A British doctor says smoking can cause "smoker's face" — a tired, wrinkled look.
☆ **1930** — birth of Claire Mackay, author of *Touching All the Bases*

Sunday 22
CBC televises a documentary on the recording of "Tears Are Not Enough," the video made by Canadian musicians to raise money for Ethiopian famine relief.
☆ **1969** — birth of Myriam Bedard, champion biathlete

Monday 23
Tourists check out the 1818th star on Hollywood's Walk of Fame. Bugs Bunny, the world's most famous rabbit, pressed his "foot" into wet concrete on Saturday.
☆ **1908** — birth of Yousuf Karsh, photographer

Tuesday 24
Canadians learn they'll be paying about $14 million for the Christmas cards and brochures their members of parliament mailed to them this year.

Wednesday 25
Christmas
The last ocean-going ship makes it safely out of the St. Lawrence Seaway before the ice closes up the system for winter.
☆ **1955?** — birth of Allanah Myles, singer-songwriter

Thursday 26
Carling Bassett, Canada's top tennis player, is the Canadian Press female athlete of the year.

Friday 27
Rap music is moving into the mainstream, with groups like the Beastie Boys, LL Cool J and Run-DMC getting more and more air play.
☆ **1823** — birth of Sir Mackenzie Bowell, fifth prime minister of Canada

Saturday 28
The word is out. The generous Santa Claus who delivered toys to 35 Port Coquitlam youngsters this Christmas was unemployed technician Rick Bertrand, who decided to share part of an $8500 accident settlement with his neighbours.
☆ **1928** — birth of Janet Lunn, co-author of *The Story of Canada*

Sunday 29
Chinese leader Deng Xiaoping is *Time* magazine's Man of the Year.

Monday 30
On Ben Johnson's birthday, sports analysts are praising this Canadian sprinter's rise to the second fastest 100-m runner in the world.

Tuesday 31
In her New Year's Day address, Governor General Jeanne Sauvé praises Canadians for their generosity and compassion during 1985.
☆ **1947** — birth of Burton Cummings, musician